First published 1981 by
Blackie and Son Limited
Bishopbriggs, Glasgow G64 2NZ
Furnival House, 14-18 High Holborn,
London WC1V 6BX

First American edition published in 1984 by
Peter Bedrick Books 125 East 23 Street · New York, N.Y. 10010

Library of Congress Cataloging in Publication Data
Hall, Amanda.
The gossipy wife.

Summary: Ivan must cure his wife of her gossiping tendency if they are to be able to keep the chest of gold coins he found in the forest.
[1. Folklore—Soviet Union. 2. Gossip—Fiction]
I. Title.
PZ8.1.H1415G o 1984 398.2′1′0947 83–15797
ISBN 0-911745-19-X
Printed in Great Britain

THE GOSSIPY WIFE

Amanda Hall

Adapted from a Russian Folk Tale

Bedrick/Blackie
New York

Long ago in Russia there lived an old man called Ivan. Though poor, he was happy and his only problem was that his wife, Katrina, was a terrible gossip. She chattered away from morning till night, wherever she was and whatever she was doing, and was quite unable to keep a secret.

One afternoon Ivan went into the forest to dig a pit to catch a wolf. He had made quite a deep hole and was just about to stop digging when suddenly his spade hit something hard. Ivan dug deeper still and at last uncovered a large, brightly coloured chest.

Cautiously he opened the lid. Inside were heaps of shimmering gold coins. Ivan could hardly believe his luck. With all this gold he and Katrina would be able to live in comfort for the rest of their days.

But then he had a worrying thought. As soon as he told Katrina about the gold she would spread the news round the village. The cruel and greedy landlord who owned the forest would soon come to hear of it and would claim all the gold for himself. How could Ivan keep the secret?

Ivan thought hard. Then suddenly an idea came to him. As soon as he had worked out his plan he buried the chest again and marked the spot with a large stone.

Then he went to check the traps which he had set earlier that day on the forest floor and in the river. Luckily, both traps had sprung. In one he had caught a hare and in the other a pike. He took the hare from its trap and placed it in the net in the river. Then he put the pike in the hare's trap.

It was dark by the time Ivan got home.

"Katrina, my dear," he said to his wife, "we've had a great stroke of luck. I've found a chest full of gold buried in the forest. We must go back and fetch it together, but it will be very heavy. Why don't you cook us some pancakes to build up our strength?"

Katrina was so excited that for once she was almost speechless. She hurried away and made a pile of pancakes. In her excitement she didn't notice that Ivan was slipping half of the pancakes into a large sack under the table.

After their meal they set off into the forest. All along the way Katrina was so busy chattering about the treasure that she didn't see Ivan hanging pancakes on the trees.

They soon reached the spot where the treasure was buried and Ivan dug up the chest. Katrina's eyes grew round at the sight of the gold. She let the coins run through her fingers. How beautifully they gleamed in the lantern's glow!

When all the gold had been loaded into the sack, Ivan said, "Let's just check the traps while we're here."

So they went to the river and Ivan pulled out the hare.

"Good gracious me!" cried Katrina. "Whatever is a hare doing in the river?"

"Silly," said Ivan. "Haven't you ever heard of water hares?" Then he led her to the pike in its trap. Again Katrina cried out in astonishment.

"Silly," said Ivan again. "It's a land pike of course! Surely you've seen one of those before."

As they walked home with their sack of gold Ivan said casually, "I see it's been raining pancakes again." He raised the lantern so that Katrina could see the pancakes hanging from the trees on either side of the path.

"Well I never!" said Katrina. "What a strange night we're having!"

On their way home they had to pass the landlord's house. Ivan walked on ahead and as he went by the landlord's gate he made a horrible screaming noise.

"What was that?" cried poor Katrina in alarm.

"Come, my dear, we must hurry home," said Ivan. "That was the landlord screaming in pain. The devil is in there wrestling with him for his soul!"

Later that night, just before he blew out the candle, Ivan warned Katrina sternly not to tell anyone about their treasure.

"Oh no, I won't say a word," promised Katrina.

But the next morning, when she met the other women at the well, Katrina just couldn't resist the temptation to gossip about the gold. How could she possibly keep such a wonderful secret to herself?

Of course the news soon reached the ears of the wicked landlord, who was furious. He sent for Ivan and Katrina at once.

"What's this I hear about you digging up treasure on *my* land?" he roared.

"Well sir, it's quite true," said Ivan. "My wife will tell you all about it."

Katrina eagerly poured out the whole story. She told the landlord about the gold and the water hare and the land pike and the shower of pancakes.

"And we felt very sorry for you, sir, when we heard you screaming as the devil tormented you."

As he listened to Katrina's ridiculous story the landlord's face grew redder and redder with rage.

"How dare you waste my time with such nonsense?" he bellowed. "Get out of my sight, both of you, and never come back!"

So that is how Ivan and Katrina were able to keep their gold and live in comfort for the rest of their days.

But as for Katrina, the gossipy wife, no one believed her stories ever again.

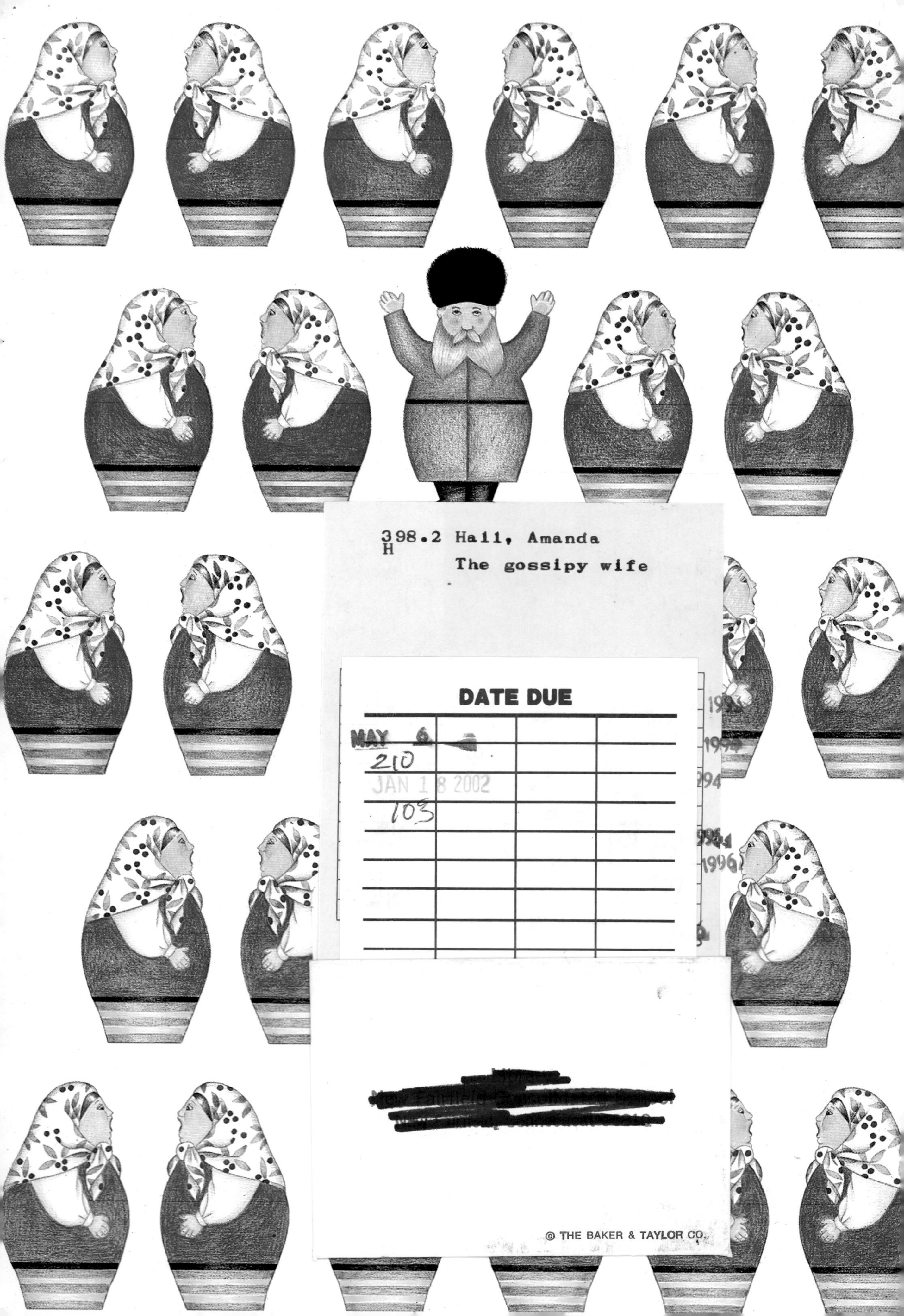
398.2 Hall, Amanda
H
The gossipy wife
DATE DUE
MAY 6
210
JAN 1 8 2002
103
© THE BAKER & TAYLOR CO.